Meet the PRESIDENT

By Michael Rajczak

Gareth Stevens
Publishing

Please visit our website, www.garethstevens.com. For a free color catalog of all our high-quality books, call toll free 1-800-542-2595 or fax 1-877-542-2596.

Library of Congress Cataloging-in-Publication Data

Rajczak, Michael.
Meet the president / Michael Rajczak.
    p. cm. — (A guide to your government)
Includes index.
ISBN 978-1-4339-7257-7 (pbk.)
ISBN 978-1-4339-7258-4 (6-pack)
ISBN 978-1-4339-7256-0 (lib. bdg.)
1. Presidents—United States—Juvenile literature. I. Title.
JK517.R35 2012
352.230973—dc23

                                    2012005873

First Edition

Published in 2013 by
Gareth Stevens Publishing
111 East 14th Street, Suite 349
New York, NY 10003

Copyright © 2013 Gareth Stevens Publishing

Designer: Daniel Hosek
Editor: Kristen Rajczak

Photo credits: Cover, p. 1 Alex Wong/Getty Images; p. 5 Mark Wilson/Getty Images; p. 7 Tom Williams/Roll Call/Getty Images; p. 9 Gaston De Cardenas/Getty Images; p. 10 Luke Frazza/AFP/Getty Images; p. 11 Henny Ray Abrams/AFP/Getty Images; p. 12 lesapi images/Shutterstock.com; pp. 13, 16, 17, 23 (Woodrow Wilson), 24, 29 (Martin Van Buren) Stock Montage/Getty Images; p. 15 (main image) Cynthia Johnson/ Time & Life Pictures/Getty Images; p. 15 (White House) Mary Terriberry/Shutterstock.com; p. 19 NASA/Science Source/Getty Images; p. 21 (Lincoln) Alexander Gardner/ Hulton Archive/Getty Images; p. 21 (Gettysburg Address) Hulton Archive/Getty Images; p. 23 (main image) SuperStock/Getty Images; p. 25 (Great Debate) Paul Schutzer/ Time & Life Pictures/Getty Images; p. 25 Keystone/Hulton Archive/Getty Images; p. 27 Benami Neaumann/Gamma-Rapho/Getty Images; p. 29 (main image) Fotosearch/ Getty Images.

Printed in the United States of America

CPSIA compliance information: Batch #CS12GS: For further information contact Gareth Stevens, New York, New York at 1-800-542-2595.

CONTENTS

Words in the glossary appear in **bold** type
the first time they are used in the text.

WHO IS THE PRESIDENT?

The president is the leader of the government of the United States of America. The president is elected by US citizens to serve a 4-year term in office. His main jobs are to enforce the laws of the country and to represent our nation around the world. Some of these duties are outlined in the US Constitution. However, far more have been added as presidents faced new challenges in a growing, changing country. These jobs are difficult and require the president's attention at all hours of the day.

The president guides our nation in matters within the country and in how our country relates to other countries. Some people consider the president of the United States the most powerful person in the world.

FEDERAL *Fact*

Each of the three branches of the federal government has a specific job. The legislative branch, Congress, makes laws. The president heads the executive branch and puts the laws into effect. The judicial branch makes sure laws are carried out correctly and legally.

Commanding US Forces

The president is the commander in chief of all US armed forces. He has the final say about sending American forces to defend the nation. He can also ask the US Congress to declare war. The last time this happened was in 1941, when Japan attacked the US naval base at Pearl Harbor in Hawaii. President Franklin Roosevelt asked Congress to declare war against Japan. A few days later, he asked Congress to declare war against Germany and Italy, too.

Barack Obama became the 44th president of the United States on January 20, 2009.

BEFORE GEORGE WASHINGTON

After the **American Revolution**, the new United States of America was governed under the Articles of Confederation. This plan for government created the office of the President of the United States in Congress Assembled. However, the role wasn't defined well. Several different men held this position. The first was a powerful member of Congress named John Hanson. Although mostly forgotten in history, his calm but firm leadership guided the new nation through uncertain times.

During his presidency, Hanson was faced with a **crisis**. The soldiers who served during the American Revolution wanted to be paid. Some soldiers came to Congress to protest, and this frightened many people in government. Some even ran away! Hanson stayed. He assured the soldiers that they would receive their pay.

FEDERAL *Fact*

When John Hanson ran for president in 1781, no one ran against him. Everyone in Congress voted for him, too—including George Washington!

A New Constitution

During the American Revolution, the 13 colonies joined together as a nation. They created a plan for one government. This plan for government was called the Articles of Confederation. Approved in 1781, the Articles of Confederation proved to be too weak of a plan to govern the nation. The federal government wasn't given much power. Representatives from the states started to write a new constitution in 1787.

Presidents of the United States in Congress Assembled, such as John Hanson, only served a 1-year term. This statue of Hanson can be found near the Capitol.

RUNNING FOR PRESIDENT

The new US Constitution created the role of president as the leader of the nation. It states that the president must be at least 35 years old and a citizen born in the United States. Presidents must have lived in the United States for at least 14 years as well.

The Constitution outlines how presidents are elected, too. A president is elected every 4 years. Today, there are usually two main candidates and a few others. The main candidates represent the Democratic and the Republican Parties. Presidential candidates often have different ideas about how the country should be run.

When an election is held, citizens cast votes for the candidate they want to win. These votes are tallied within each state. The candidate who receives the most individual votes usually wins all the electoral votes from that state.

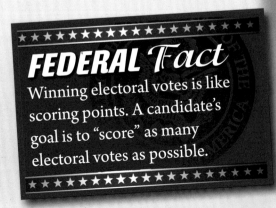

FEDERAL *Fact*

Winning electoral votes is like scoring points. A candidate's goal is to "score" as many electoral votes as possible.

The Electoral College

When citizens vote for president, they're actually voting for members of the Electoral College. Each party chooses electors to represent it. However, only electors who represent the party chosen by voters on election day become members of the Electoral College. Even though a presidential candidate may be declared a winner after the nationwide vote, it's not official until the Electoral College has cast its votes. This happens weeks after election day!

*The freedom to vote for the candidate of your choice is one of the things that makes the United States a **democracy**.*

The number of electoral votes each state has equals the number of senators and representatives it has. States with large populations have more electoral votes because they have more members in Congress. For example, California has 55 electoral votes because it has 2 senators and 53 congressmen. Seven states with small populations have only 3 electoral votes because they each have 2 senators and only 1 congressman. Washington, DC, isn't a state, but it still has 3 electoral votes.

In 2000, George W. Bush defeated Al Gore for the presidency when he won the most electoral votes. However, Gore won the nationwide *popular vote*.

Al Gore

George W. Bush

Altogether, there are 538 electoral votes. The candidate who receives the majority of the electoral votes becomes president. This means that a candidate must receive at least 270 electoral votes. There have been four times in US history when the candidate who won the nationwide popular vote didn't win the electoral vote.

Tiebreaker

It's possible that there could be a tie for the number of electoral votes, 269–269. If that happens, the Constitution says that the tie will be broken by a vote in the House of Representatives. Each state only gets one vote in this election. The candidate who receives the most votes becomes the new president. The House will also choose the president if no one candidate receives the proper majority of votes needed.

While some newspapers declared Bush the winner of the 2000 election right away, others stated their doubt in the close vote count.

OUR FIRST PRESIDENT

George Washington was the first president of the United States. He was a strong general who led the 13 colonies to victory in the American Revolution. Because of his bravery on the battlefield and his work as president of the **Constitutional Convention**, Washington had the respect of his countrymen. He served his two presidential terms in New York City while making plans for a new capital city.

As president, Washington believed that his first responsibility was to keep the nation safe. When Britain and France went to war, he kept our nation out of the conflict. Washington also wanted the country to be strong at home. He created policies to handle the nation's money. He also insisted that states and citizens follow the nation's laws.

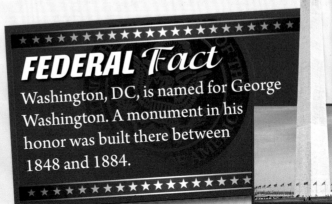

FEDERAL *Fact*

Washington, DC, is named for George Washington. A monument in his honor was built there between 1848 and 1884.

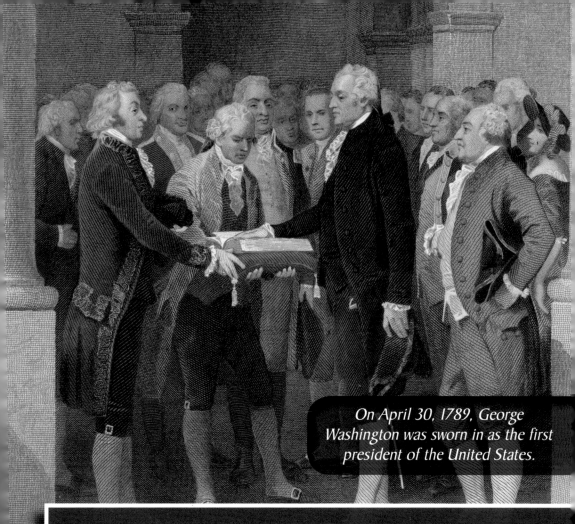

On April 30, 1789, George Washington was sworn in as the first president of the United States.

Choosing the Vice President

After the Constitution was approved, a president needed to be elected. George Washington received the most electoral votes and was declared president in 1789. John Adams received the second-highest number of votes and was named vice president. This way of deciding who would be vice president remained until 1804, when a Constitutional amendment passed. It stated that votes for vice presidential candidates would be cast separately from those for presidential candidates.

THE PRESIDENT'S JOB

The president takes on many duties after he is elected. The US Constitution assigns some of these duties. In addition to acting as commander in chief of the armed forces, the president appoints federal judges and other officials. He can sign bills into law or **veto** those he thinks aren't good for the nation. The president also directs the United States' relations with other countries, including signing treaties and meeting with the heads of other nations. The Constitution gives the president the power to pardon criminals, too.

The president is helped by a group of advisors called the cabinet. Members of the cabinet include the vice president and the heads of the 15 executive departments. These include the secretary of state, the secretary of defense, and the attorney general.

FEDERAL Fact

The president can only pardon federal criminals. This may mean the offender is released from prison, but more often they just receive a lesser punishment.

The White House

The president's home and office are in the White House, located at 1600 Pennsylvania Avenue in Washington, DC. The West Wing of the White House  contains the Oval Office, an oval-shaped room that has the president's desk. Here, he often meets with advisors. The Oval Office is a common place for the president to give televised speeches, too. Among the 132 rooms in the White House, there are 35 bathrooms, 28 fireplaces, and 8 staircases.

Most presidents have been married and their spouses often offer advice, too. Here, Hillary Clinton speaks to her husband, President Bill Clinton, at an event in 1997.

15

PRESIDENTS GUIDE GROWTH

The president's job has expanded as events have unfolded in history. In 1803, the United States' western border was the Mississippi River. France owned the port city of New Orleans at the mouth of the Mississippi River, which the United States wanted to use. The country approached France with a deal to buy it. When France offered New Orleans and the whole Louisiana Territory, President Thomas Jefferson agreed. His actions expanded presidential power to include adding new lands.

The presidential veto has changed over time, too. In 1832, President Andrew Jackson vetoed a new plan for the national bank, which he said favored the rich. Before this, presidents only vetoed a bill when they were concerned with its constitutionality. Jackson used it to show political position as well as constitutional concern.

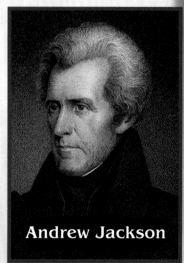

Andrew Jackson

The Louisiana Purchase doubled the size of the United States.

Louisiana Purchase

United States in 1803

The Louisiana Purchase doubled the size of the United States.

FEDERAL *Fact*

The Louisiana Purchase set the stage for other lands to be added to the United States. Texas, following a war for its independence from Mexico, was added in 1845.

The Power of Veto

When Congress is in session, the president has 10 days to sign or veto a bill. If he does neither, the bill becomes law without his signature. However, when Congress isn't in session, the president can simply not sign a bill, rejecting it without using a formal veto. This is called a pocket veto, as if the president put the bill in his pocket and forgot about it!

17

PRESIDENTS INSPIRE US

Although it's not specifically part of their job description, many presidents inspire people with their words and deeds. George Washington had been a strong leader as the commander in chief of the Continental army during the American Revolution. Some people wanted to make him King George I of America! He rejected the idea, even retiring as general by handing his sword to the members of Congress. When elected president, he chose his words and actions carefully, knowing he was setting a precedent for future presidents.

Other presidents have inspired the nation by leading the United States through wars and hard times. Some made great speeches that have been remembered. A speech by John F. Kennedy helped inspire the nation to put a man on the moon!

FEDERAL Fact

A precedent is an example that others follow. Because George Washington served two terms as president, presidents until Franklin Roosevelt served no more than two terms. After Roosevelt's four terms, an amendment passed, limiting presidents to two terms.

President John F. Kennedy gives a speech at Rice University in 1962.

Kennedy Inspired Action

"Ask not what your country can do for you. Ask what you can do for your country." President Kennedy spoke these words during his Inaugural Address, or the speech given when a president is sworn in to office. He inspired thousands of Americans to serve their nation in a variety of ways. This included joining the Peace Corps, an organization Kennedy established that sends people to work on projects abroad as representatives of the United States.

19

LINCOLN: LIBERATOR AND LEADER

There has been no greater crisis for the United States than the Civil War and perhaps no more inspiring president than Abraham Lincoln, who helped US unity prevail. Issues concerning states' rights and slavery created deep differences between Northern and Southern states. Lincoln was elected in 1860 without even being a choice on Southern ballots. Feeling they no longer had a say in government, Southern states began leaving the Union.

Lincoln was determined to keep the nation together. After Southern forces attacked US troops, he sent the army into the South. Four bloody and bitter years of fighting followed. During the war, Lincoln issued the Emancipation Proclamation. This ended slavery in the rebel Southern states. Guided by Lincoln, the North won the war, and the United States remained one nation.

FEDERAL *Fact*
Eleven states **seceded** from the United States. They set up their own country called the Confederate States of America.

During Lincoln's second term, Congress passed an amendment outlawing slavery in the United States. By the end of the war, all slaves were free.

The Gettysburg Address

Abraham Lincoln gave a famous speech when dedicating the battlefield at Gettysburg, Pennsylvania, as a national cemetery. He said: "… that these dead shall not have died in vain—that this nation, under God, shall have a new birth of freedom—and that government of the people, by the people, for the people, shall not perish from the earth." Some people consider Lincoln the greatest US president.

draft of the Gettysburg Address

LEADING US THROUGH WARS

During wartime, a president is called upon to make important decisions. He often will talk to advisors and experts before making difficult choices. As commander in chief of the nation's armed forces, a president's leadership can determine the outcome of a war.

When World War I broke out in Europe in 1914, the United States wanted to stay out of the conflict at first. Then, in April 1917, President Woodrow Wilson asked Congress to join the war because Germany was attacking American ships. Because of the help of the United States, the British and French were victorious.

The president's role in wartime also includes informing the American people about current and future strategies. He often gives speeches of hope and encouragement to both citizens at home and those in the military.

FEDERAL *Fact*

Presidents' actions as commander in chief often have far-reaching effects. President James K. Polk chose to **annex** Texas, which led to war with Mexico.

This photograph from 1917 shows President Woodrow Wilson addressing Congress and asking them to join World War I.

War in the 20th and 21st Centuries

Since the two world wars, presidents have led our nation into conflicts they felt were important to the nation's interests. President Lyndon Johnson increased the numbers of US soldiers in the **Vietnam War**. President George W. Bush sent troops into Afghanistan and Iraq following the **terrorist** attacks on September 11, 2001. However, US military goals greatly vary from one president to the next. The presidents who followed both Johnson and Bush won election partially on promises to bring US troops home.

23

ADDRESSING THE NATION

According to the Constitution, each president is required to give an accounting of our nation to Congress. These accounts are now known as the State of the Union, a phrase coined by President Franklin Roosevelt in 1935. At first, the president's addresses were reported only in newspapers. But as technology has improved, so have the ways the president communicates with the nation.

In 1922, President Warren G. Harding became the first president to be heard on the radio. Soon, candidates for president started using radio addresses to reach out to voters. During the 1960 presidential election, candidate **debates** began to be shown on television. These "Great Debates" famously helped John F. Kennedy defeat Richard M. Nixon.

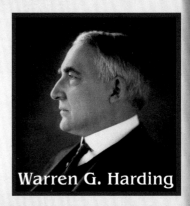

Warren G. Harding

FEDERAL *Fact*

President Barack Obama became the first president to make extensive use of the Internet while running for president in 2008.

The President on TV

Franklin Roosevelt was the first president on TV when he addressed the opening of the World's Fair in 1939. Since then, presidents have used televised addresses in many ways. In October 1962, President John F. Kennedy addressed the nation on television to explain that the Soviet Union was trying to place missiles in Cuba. President George W. Bush took to the airwaves in 2003 to let the nation know that the United States had invaded Iraq.

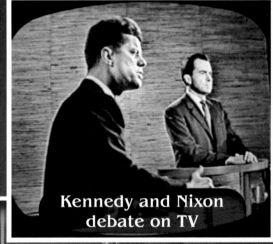

Kennedy and Nixon debate on TV

During the Great Depression, a time of economic crisis when nearly one-third of the nation didn't have jobs, President Franklin Roosevelt, shown below, gave weekly addresses to keep the nation informed and to provide encouragement. These addresses became known as his "fireside chats."

THE PRESIDENT AND THE WORLD

Presidents and their decisions have affected the entire world. While not every decision is popular, many people believe it's part of the US president's job to set an example for other countries.

In 1905, President Theodore Roosevelt mediated talks to end a war between Russia and Japan. Around the same time, he also guided the building of the Panama Canal, a waterway allowing easier travel between the Atlantic and the Pacific Oceans. After World War I, President Woodrow Wilson traveled to Europe to guide the treaty talks that ended the war and to create a **League of Nations**. Although Wilson couldn't convince the United States to join the league, his vision led President Franklin Roosevelt to help create a stronger organization, the **United Nations**, in 1945.

FEDERAL *Fact*

In 1945, President Harry S. Truman made the decision to use two atomic bombs to end World War II. This caused extreme damage to Japan and began the age of nuclear weapons.

President Jimmy Carter congratulates the leaders of Egypt and Israel on a peace agreement in 1979. Carter had a key role in the talks between the two nations.

The President Works with the UN

When **Communists** from northern Korea invaded southern Korea in 1950, President Truman went to the United Nations. He asked that the UN help the United States support the legally elected government in southern Korea. The fighting that followed became known as the Korean Conflict. Truman's approach began a tradition of US presidents working with other nations through the UN to solve problems around the world.

PRESIDENTIAL FIRSTS

Since George Washington took office in 1789, the US presidency has grown into one of the most important leadership roles in the world. However, just as Washington set the first precedents, each president has made his mark on the job. Here are some presidential firsts that changed the US presidency in big and small ways:

- **James K. Polk** (1845–1849) was the first president to have his photograph taken while in office.

- **William Henry Harrison** (1881) was the first president to die in office. He was only president for 1 month!

- **Theodore Roosevelt** (1901–1909) was the first president to travel outside the country while in office.

- **Richard M. Nixon** (1969–1974) became the first and only president to resign from office.

- **Gerald Ford** (1974–1977) became the first man to serve as president without being elected as either president or vice president. He took the place of Nixon's vice president, who resigned, and then became president when Nixon resigned.

28

Theodore Roosevelt visited Panama in 1906. Today, the president travels all over the world.

Theodore Roosevelt

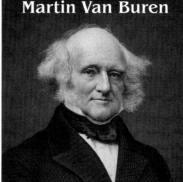

Martin Van Buren

Born in the USA

Martin Van Buren was the first president who was born in the United States. Earlier presidents had all been born before the American Revolution. They were originally citizens of Great Britain living in the American colonies.

GLOSSARY

American Revolution: the war in which the colonies won their freedom from England (1775–1783)

annex: to take over an area and make it part of a larger territory

Communist: a person who follows Communism, a system of beliefs in which people share their property and goods

Constitutional Convention: the meeting in 1787 at which state representatives helped write the Constitution

crisis: a situation in which events are very difficult or uncertain and action must be taken to avoid disaster

debate: to discuss an issue by presenting all sides. Also, the discussion itself.

democracy: a system of government in which leaders are chosen by the citizens

League of Nations: a group of nations that united after World War I to try to peacefully settle conflicts between nations. The league was replaced by the United Nations.

popular vote: the combined individual votes of all citizens who cast a vote

secede: to leave a country

terrorist: one who uses violence and fear to challenge an authority

United Nations: a group of nations that united after World War II with the intention of resolving conflicts between nations

veto: the president's power to stop something from becoming law. Also, to reject.

Vietnam War: a conflict starting in 1955 and ending in 1975 between South Vietnam and North Vietnam in which the United States joined with South Vietnam

FOR MORE INFORMATION

Books

Bausum, Ann. *Our Country's Presidents: All You Need to Know About the Presidents, from George Washington to Barack Obama*. Washington, DC: National Geographic, 2009.

Kowalski, Kathiann M. *Checks and Balances: A Look at the Powers of Government*. Minneapolis, MN: Lerner Publications, 2012.

Schuh, Mari C. *The U.S. Presidency*. Mankato, MN: Capstone Press, 2011.

Websites

George Washington Loved Ice Cream—and Other US Presidential Fun Facts
kids.nationalgeographic.com/kids/stories/peopleplaces/georgewashingtonicecream/
Read many fun facts about the presidents and find links to videos, games, and more information about the presidents.

Presidents: The Secret History
pbskids.org/wayback/
Play games to learn more about how US presidents are elected and other interesting facts.

INDEX